W9-DAG-771

36 ft

30 ft

24 ft

18 ft

12 ft

6 ft

:eratops   Tyrannosaurus rex   Velociraptor

Dinosaurs

Arnaud Plumeri • Story
Bloz • Art
Maëla Cosson • Color

New York

Dinesaurs Graphic Novels Available from PAPERCUTZ™

Graphic Novel #1
"In the Beginning…"

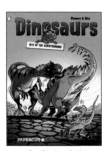
Graphic Novel #2
"Bite of the Albertosaurus"

Graphic Novel #3
"Jurassic Smarts"

DINOSAURS 3-D

Graphic Novel #4
"A Game of Bones"

Welcome, dino buffs!

In the jokes you're about to read, we've tried to work with the latest scientific understanding about dinosaurs as much as possible…all the while realizing that not a week goes by without new revelations about the "terrible lizards." Indeed, who would have believed some years ago that the famous Velociraptor had feathers?

Put on your backpack, and let's go follow the oddest creatures the earth has ever known!

The authors

Thank you, Bloz and Maela! You brought the dinosaurs I have in my head to life!

Thank you to our super readers: stay curious your whole lives!

And thank you to paleontologists for their support, particularly Ronan Allain, Andrea Cau, Cristiano Dal Sasso, Dinosaur George, Andrew Farke, and Thomas Holtz. I dedicate this volume to Marcel Gotlib and to my twinosaurs, Arthur and Heloise.

Arnaud

DINOSAURS graphic novels are available for $10.99 only in hardcover. Available from booksellers everywhere. You can also order online from papercutz.com. Or call 1-800-886-1223, Monday through Friday, 9 – 5 EST. MC, Visa, and AmEx accepted. To order by mail, please add $4.00 for postage and handling for first book ordered, $1.00 for each additional book and make check payable to NBM Publishing. Send to: Papercutz, 160 Broadway, Suite 700, East Wing, New York, NY 10038.

DINOSAURS graphic novels are also available digitally wherever e-books are sold.

Papercutz.com

Dinesaurs

Les Dinosaures [Dinosaurs] by Arnaud Plumeri & Bloz © 2012 BAMBOO ÉDITION.
www.bamboo.fr
All other editorial material © 2015 by Papercutz.

DINOSAURS #4
"A Game of Bones"

Arnaud Plumeri – Writer
Bloz – Artist
Maëla Cosson – Colorist
Nanette McGuinness – Translation
Janice Chiang – Letterer
Dani Breckenridge – Editorial Intern
Jeff Whitman – Production Coordinator
Bethany Bryan – Editor
Jim Salicrup
Editor-in-Chief

ISBN: 978-1-62991-282-0

Printed in China
August 2015 by WKT Co. LTD
3/F Phase I Leader Industrial Centre
188 Texaco Road, Tseun Wan, N.T., Hong Kong

Papercutz books may be purchased for business or promotional use. For information on bulk purchases please contact Macmillan Corporate and Premium Sales Department at (800) 221-7945 x5442.

Distributed by Macmillan
First Papercutz Printing

ICHTHYOVENATOR

YOU KNOW ABOUT SPINOSAURUS, AN AFRICAN DINOSAUR BIGGER THAN THE T. REX.

YOU SAW ME WHUP HIM IN JURASSIC PARK 3!

IMAGINE! ONE OF ITS STRANGE COUSINS HAS BEEN DISCOVERED IN LAOS!

YUP! HE'S SO WEIRD WE DON'T INVITE HIM TO FAMILY REUNIONS ANYMORE!

THE CHARACTER IN QUESTION: ICHTHYOVENATOR...

LET'S TAKE A LOOK...

THIS DINOSAUR IS AN ARTIST... IN THE FIELD OF FISHING!

:BURP!: I'M FULL.

YOUR DINOSAUR IS ABSOLUTELY HIDEOUS...

WAS HE EATEN BY MOTHS, OR WHAT? HE'S GOT A BIG HOLE IN HIS SAIL!

SAY WHAT?!

UMM... NOTHING, NOTHING!

LET ME REMIND YOU THAT YOU'RE NOT HUNGRY ANYMORE.

WE WONDER TODAY WHAT THAT HOLE WAS FOR... HERE'S ONE HYPOTHESIS!

YOU'RE RIGHT! ALLEY-OOP! INTO MY HOLE! YOU'LL BE MY SNACK!

HELP!

ICHTHYOVENATOR

MEANING: FISH HUNTER
PERIOD: EARLY CRETACEOUS (112-125 MILLION YEARS AGO)
ORDER/ FAMILY: SAURISCHIA/ SPINOSAURIDAE
SIZE: 27 FEET LONG (8 METERS)
WEIGHT: 1 TON (907KG)
DIET: PISCIVORE
FOUND: LAOS

THE SPRINTER

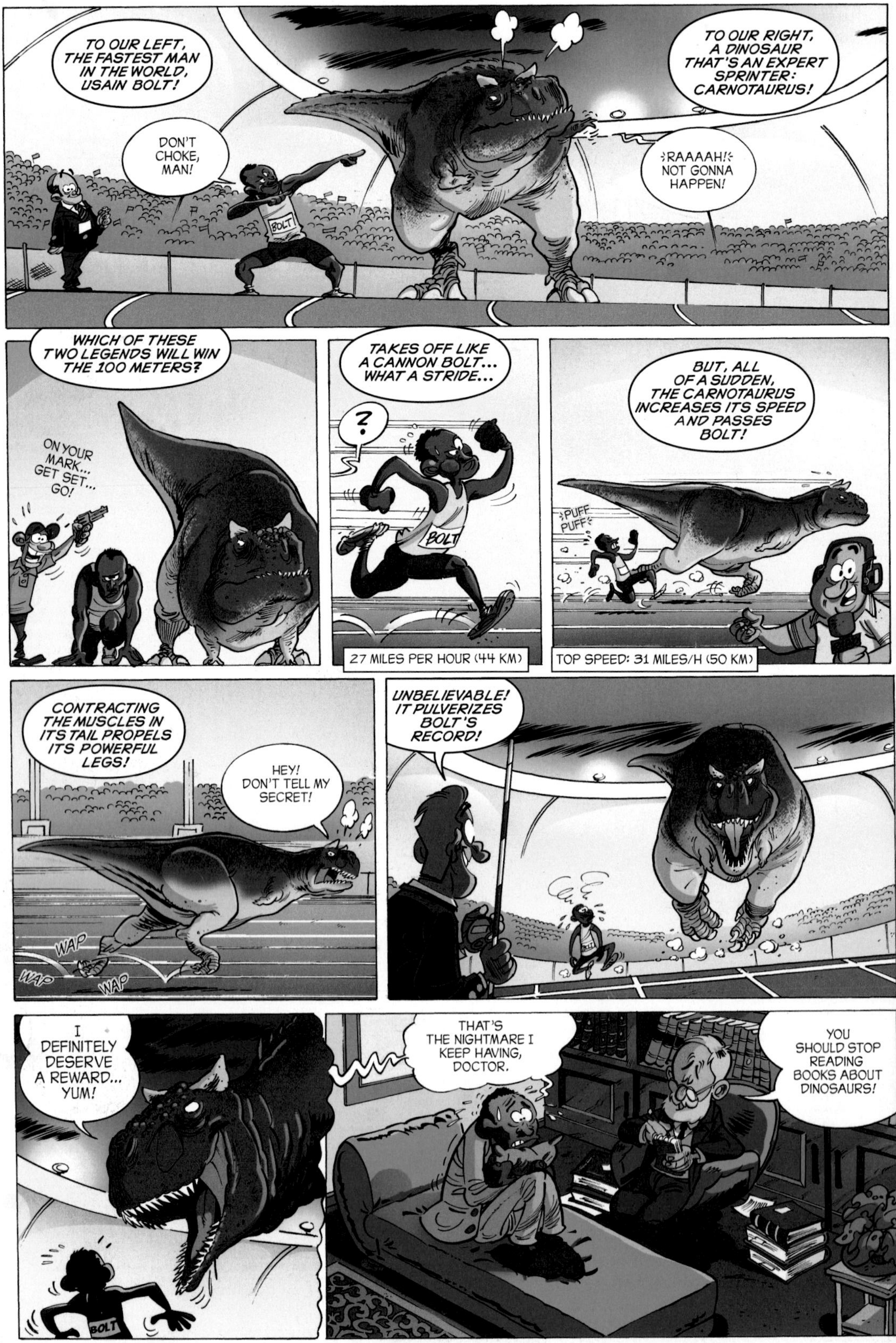

TO OUR LEFT, THE FASTEST MAN IN THE WORLD, USAIN BOLT!
TO OUR RIGHT, A DINOSAUR THAT'S AN EXPERT SPRINTER: CARNOTAURUS!
DON'T CHOKE, MAN!
¡RAAAAH!¡ NOT GONNA HAPPEN!
BOLT
WHICH OF THESE TWO LEGENDS WILL WIN THE 100 METERS?
ON YOUR MARK... GET SET... GO!
TAKES OFF LIKE A CANNON BOLT... WHAT A STRIDE...
?
BOLT
27 MILES PER HOUR (44 KM)
BUT, ALL OF A SUDDEN, THE CARNOTAURUS INCREASES ITS SPEED AND PASSES BOLT!
PUFF PUFF
TOP SPEED: 31 MILES/H (50 KM)
CONTRACTING THE MUSCLES IN ITS TAIL PROPELS ITS POWERFUL LEGS!
HEY! DON'T TELL MY SECRET!
WAP
WAP
WAP
UNBELIEVABLE! IT PULVERIZES BOLT'S RECORD!
I DEFINITELY DESERVE A REWARD... YUM!
BOLT
THAT'S THE NIGHTMARE I KEEP HAVING, DOCTOR.
YOU SHOULD STOP READING BOOKS ABOUT DINOSAURS!

THE DINOSAUR THAT NEVER EXISTED

I RECEIVED A LETTER FROM MARCEL GOTLIB WHO ASKS...

— HMM...

..."DEAR INDINO JONES, WOULD IT HAVE BEEN POSSIBLE TO BE CRUSHED BY A BRONTOSAURUS IN THE MIDDLE OF THE JURASSIC PERIOD?"

THE ANSWER IS, "NO!"

OH, YEAH? WORKS FOR ME!

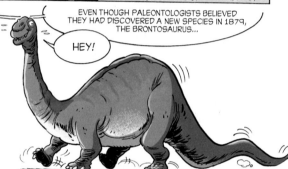

EVEN THOUGH PALEONTOLOGISTS BELIEVED THEY HAD DISCOVERED A NEW SPECIES IN 1879, THE BRONTOSAURUS...

HEY!

THEIR DINOSAUR ACTUALLY CONSISTED OF THE BODY OF AN APATOSAURUS AND THE HEAD OF A CAMARASAURUS.

IMPOSTER!

GIVE US BACK OUR BONES!

BAH?

EXACTLY!

:OOF!: IF I'VE UNDERSTOOD COMPLETELY, THE BRONTOSAURUS DIDN'T EXIST?!

...BUT THE 30-TON APATOSAURUS DEFINITELY EXISTED!

:ARGGH!:

:SPLAT:

APATOSAURUS

MEANING: DECEPTIVE REPTILE
PERIOD: LATE JURASSIC (150-155 MILLION YEARS AGO)
ORDER/ FAMILY: SAURISCHIA/ DIPLODOCIDAE
SIZE: 28 YARDS LONG (26 METERS)
WEIGHT: 30 TONS (27,216 KG)
DIET: HERBIVORE
FOUND: UNITED STATES

See page 47 for an urgent BRONTOSAURUS UPDATE!

THE BIGGEST ANIMAL

THERE HAVE BEEN SOME PRETTY BIG BEASTS ON THE EARTH, FOR EXAMPLE...

THE BIGGEST TERRESTRIAL ANIMAL ALIVE, THE AFRICAN ELEPHANT, WEIGHS AROUND 7 TONS!

THE PARACERATHERIUM, AN EXTINCT MAMMAL, COULD REACH 18 TONS.

AMONG DINOSAURS, ARGENTINOSAURUS WOULD HAVE UNDOUBTEDLY WEIGHED 88 TONS!

?

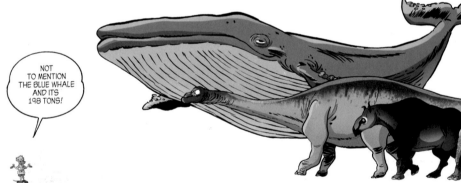

NOT TO MENTION THE BLUE WHALE AND ITS 198 TONS!

THUS, TO ANSWER YOUR QUESTION...

IF THESE CREATURES AREN'T WORRIED ABOUT THEIR WEIGHT, NEITHER SHOULD YOU.

WHY ARE YOU IN MY BATHROOM?

ACROCANTHOSAURUS VS. DEINONYCHUS

COME LOOK, TENONTOSAURUS! THERE'S A BIG SHOW TODAY!

THE DEINONYCHUS ARE PICKING A FIGHT WITH THE ACROCANTHOSAURS.

RWAR!

RRWEEE

GROOOOW...

ROOOOOO...

THE ACROCANTHOSAURUS IS A 40-FOOT MONSTER WITH SHARP TEETH AND CLAWS...

THE DEINONYCHUS MAY BE ORGANIZED RAPTORS, BUT THEY STILL DON'T HAVE A CHANCE.

ROAR

RWEEE   RWEEEK

SNAP!

BECAUSE THE ACROCANTHOSAURUS IS USED TO HUNTING 100-FOOT GIANTS

GET AWAY FROM ME, YOU LITTLE FLEABAGS!

THEY'RE REALLY AWESOME! I'M SUCH A FAN!

BY THE WAY, WHY ARE THEY FIGHTING?

WELL...

...TO FIGURE OUT WHO HAS THE RIGHT TO DEVOUR YOU!

HE'S OURS! WE SAW HIM FIRST!

IN YOUR DREAMS! THAT'S MY TENONTOSAURUS!

ACROCANTHOSAURUS

MEANING: HIGH-SPINE LIZARD
PERIOD: EARLY CRETACEOUS (110–116 MILLION YEARS AGO)
ORDER/ FAMILY: SAURISCHIA/ CARCHARAODONTOSAURIDAE
SIZE: 40 FEET LONG (12 METERS)
WEIGHT: 7 TONS (6350 KILOGRAMS)
DIET: CARNIVORE
FOUND: UNITED STATES (OKLAHOMA, TEXAS, UTAH)

PLUMERI & BLOZ

PEGOMASTAX

IN ORDER TO SURVIVE, THE SMALL MAMMALS HAVE NO CHOICE...

WE HAVE TO BE QUIET!

THEY TAKE ADVANTAGE OF THE DARK TO LOOK FOR FOOD.

GREAT TO EAT!

TOUGH LUCK! THE MOST TERRIBLE DINOSAUR IS ALSO OUT AND ABOUT...

WATCH OUT! ♪NYUCK! NYUCK!♪

AND IT'S HUNGRY, TOO!

OOOOOH!

WHAT'S MORE, SOME PEOPLE CLAIM IT'S A VAMPIRE!

HSSSSS

ITS NAME: PEGOMASTAX!

♪HSSSSS!♪ THAT NICE MEAL'S MINE!

THIS TIME, WE'RE DONE FOR!

WE THINK, HOWEVER, PEGOMASTAX ONLY ATE FRUIT AND NUTS...

OUR PINE CONE! THIEF!

DELICIOUSH!

CRACK CRACK

PEGOMASTAX

MEANING: STRONG JAW
PERIOD: EARLY JURASSIC (183-200 MILLION YEARS AGO)
ORDER/ FAMILY: ORNITHISCHIA/ HETERODONTOSAURIDAE
SIZE: 2 FEET (60 CENTIMETERS LONG)
WEIGHT: 55 POUNDS (25 KG)
DIET: HERBIVORE
FOUND: SOUTH AFRICA

OH, NO! WITH ALL THESE PEOPLE, I WON'T GET NEAR MY IDOL!

INDY! INDY! THE NEXT SEQUEL! WE WANT THE NEXT ADVENTURE!

MEET INDIANA JONES

WHILE WE WAIT, I'LL TELL YOU THE STORY THAT INSPIRED INDIANA JONES...

IT ISN'T ABOUT ME, EH! IT'S ABOUT ROY CHAPMAN ANDREWS!

THANK GOODNESS.

HE WAS READY TO DO ANYTHING TO BECOME A PALEONTOLOGIST AND APPLIED TO WORK AT THE MNH* IN 1906...

I WANT TO FIND LOTS OF FOSSILS AND MAKE THE MUSEUM SHINE THROUGHOUT THE WORLD!

*MUSEUM OF NATURAL HISTORY IN NEW YORK

MAKE THE MUSEUM SHINE? HERE, TAKE THIS AND MOP THE FLOOR WITH IT!

BUT THEY SUGGESTED HE BEGIN AS A JANITOR!

WITH TIME, HE WOUND UP BECOMING ONE OF THE MUSEUM'S MAIN DIRECTORS.

YOUR MISSION: FIND PREHISTORIC CREATURES IN THE GOBI DESERT.

⸓WOO HOO!⸓ I'LL GRAB MY WHIP, AND IT'S OFF TO THE GOBI!

BETWEEN 1922 AND 1930, HE LED A MAMMOTH CONVOY THROUGH THE HEART OF MONGOLIA...

WE'VE GOT 8 VEHICLES, 40 MEN, 150 CAMELS...

...AND NO ONE THOUGHT TO BRING ANY SUNSCREEN?!

A VERY RISKY JOURNEY, IN A HOSTILE ENVIRONMENT. NIGHTS IN MONGOLIA ARE COLD...

I'VE GOT A BAD FEELING ABOUT THIS...

...AS A RESULT, SNAKES TAKE REFUGE IN THE TENTS!

⸓ARGH!⸓ I HATE SNAKES!

BAM BAM

HSSS

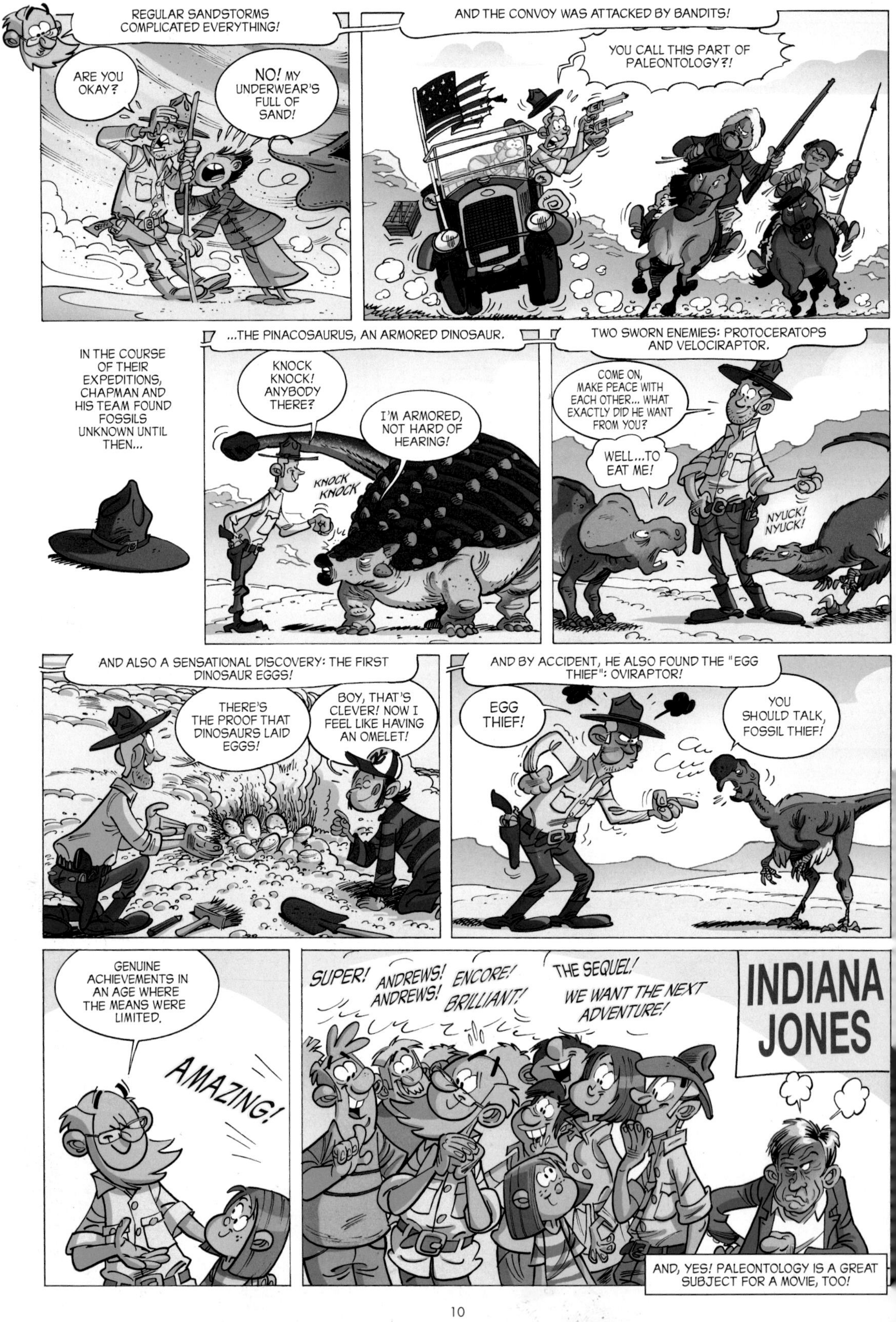
REGULAR SANDSTORMS COMPLICATED EVERYTHING!
ARE YOU OKAY?
NO! MY UNDERWEAR'S FULL OF SAND!
AND THE CONVOY WAS ATTACKED BY BANDITS!
YOU CALL THIS PART OF PALEONTOLOGY?!
IN THE COURSE OF THEIR EXPEDITIONS, CHAPMAN AND HIS TEAM FOUND FOSSILS UNKNOWN UNTIL THEN...
...THE PINACOSAURUS, AN ARMORED DINOSAUR.
KNOCK KNOCK! ANYBODY THERE?
KNOCK KNOCK
I'M ARMORED, NOT HARD OF HEARING!
TWO SWORN ENEMIES: PROTOCERATOPS AND VELOCIRAPTOR.
COME ON, MAKE PEACE WITH EACH OTHER... WHAT EXACTLY DID HE WANT FROM YOU?
WELL...TO EAT ME!
NYUCK! NYUCK!
AND ALSO A SENSATIONAL DISCOVERY: THE FIRST DINOSAUR EGGS!
THERE'S THE PROOF THAT DINOSAURS LAID EGGS!
BOY, THAT'S CLEVER! NOW I FEEL LIKE HAVING AN OMELET!
AND BY ACCIDENT, HE ALSO FOUND THE "EGG THIEF": OVIRAPTOR!
EGG THIEF!
YOU SHOULD TALK, FOSSIL THIEF!
GENUINE ACHIEVEMENTS IN AN AGE WHERE THE MEANS WERE LIMITED.
AMAZING!
SUPER!
ANDREWS! ANDREWS!
ENCORE! BRILLIANT!
THE SEQUEL!
WE WANT THE NEXT ADVENTURE!
INDIANA JONES
AND, YES! PALEONTOLOGY IS A GREAT SUBJECT FOR A MOVIE, TOO!

DINOSAUR COLORS

FOR A LONG TIME, WE THOUGHT IT WAS IMPOSSIBLE TO KNOW THE COLOR OF DINOSAURS...

BAH, YES... THEY TURN ALL PALE WHEN THEY SEE ME!

THANKS TO PROGRESS IN SCIENCE, WE HAVE CLUES ABOUT A NUMBER OF FEATHERED DINOSAURS...

AND DINOSAURS WITHOUT FEATHERS, THEN? STILL FORGOTTEN?

I'M GREEN WITH ENVY!

BECAUSE WE DISCOVERED "MELANOSOMES," MICROSCOPIC COLOR PIGMENTS.

AREN'T WE A BUNCH OF COLORFUL CHARACTERS?

THAT'S LAME!

THE RESULT: WE THINK THAT SINOSAUROPTERYX WAS A HANDSOME GINGER.

INJURE?! WHO, ME?

NO, A GINGER. HE HAS A RED HEAD.

ARCHEOPTERYX WOULD ACTUALLY HAVE BEEN BLACK AND WHITE, LIKE A MAGPIE.

LIKE A CHICKEN IN A TUXEDO!

WHAT'S THIS NEW SWANKY LOOK?

JUST AS ANOTHER DINOSAUR-BIRD, ANCHIORNIS, WOULD HAVE HAD AN ORANGEY CREST.

⸮PHOOEY!⸮ YOU DIDN'T EVEN NOTICE MY NEW COLOR!

IT'S ALL OVER BETWEEN US!

BUT--

BUT WHAT DO OUR T. REX FRIENDS THINK OF THESE STORIES ABOUT COLORS?

⸮YUCK!⸮ I ATE A GREEN ONE; IT WASN'T VERY RIPE!

⸮YUM!⸮ THE RED ONES ARE VERY SWEET!

ON THE OTHER HAND, THE BLUE ONES ARE TOO SPICY!

THIS IS MAKING ME HUNGRY!

NANOTYRANNUS

NO WAY! COME TAKE A LOOK!

?

SOME THINK IT'S A DWARF SPECIES FROM THE LARGE FAMILY OF TYRANNOSAURS.

WE'RE OBVIOUSLY DEALING WITH A SEPARATE SPECIES, NANOTYRANNUS!

PAT, PAT, PAT

OTHERS MAINTAIN THAT IT'S JUST A YOUNG T. REX.

NOT AT ALL! IT'S A T. REX THAT'S NOT YET AN ADULT!

?

IT'S ABSOLUTELY NOT A T. REX! LOOK, IT HAS FEWER TEETH!

I'M TELLING YOU, THE SKULLS OF THESE DINOSAURS CHANGE AS THEY GROW!

THE EASIEST THING WOULD BE TO ASK A T. REX...

IS IT A LITTLE T. REX? WE'LL HAVE TO LOOK...

ROAR!

OOPS!

CHOMP

YIKES!

FEEEEK!

DUNNO IF IT'S OURS...

...BUT WE DON'T WANT A BLOCKHEAD LIKE THAT AROUND HERE!

IT'S STILL A MYSTERY!

NANOTYRANNUS

MEANING: DWARF TYRANT
PERIOD: LATE CRETACEOUS (65 MILLION YEARS AGO)
ORDER/ FAMILY: SAURISCHIA/ TYRANNOSAURIDAE
SIZE: 20 FEET (6 METERS LONG)
WEIGHT: 2205 POUNDS (1 METRIC TON)
DIET: CARNIVORE
FOUND: UNITED STATES (MONTANA)

THE HADROSAURUS FESTIVAL

DINOSAURS DATING

SO WHEN ARE WE GOING TO SEE SOME DINOSAURS, SIR?

WE'RE GOING TO SEE SOMETHING EVEN BETTER THAN DINOSAURS: ROCKS THAT GO BACK IN TIME!

BOOOOO...

BUT LOOK! ROCKS ARE COOL! THEY LET US DATE WHEN EACH DINOSAUR LIVED...

IMAGINE, A DINOSAUR STRETCHED ALONG THE GROUND...

COUGH! COUGH!

IT'S THE END FOR ME...

NEVER FORGET ME, GUYS...

...WHICH ARE COVERED BY COUNTLESS LAYERS OF SAND AND CLAY...

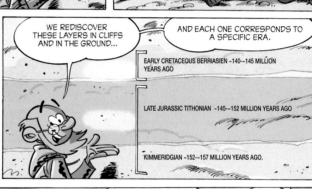

WE REDISCOVER THESE LAYERS IN CLIFFS AND IN THE GROUND...

AND EACH ONE CORRESPONDS TO A SPECIFIC ERA.

EARLY CRETACEOUS BERRIASIEN ~140-~145 MILLION YEARS AGO

LATE JURASSIC TITHONIAN ~145-~152 MILLION YEARS AGO

KIMMERIDGIAN ~152-~157 MILLION YEARS AGO.

IF A BONE IS FOUND IN ONE OF THESE LAYERS, WE THEN KNOW WHEN IT DATES BACK TO.

SCRATCH SCRATCH

SO ARE MY ROCKS STILL WORTHLESS?

?!!!

YOUR ROCKS ARE TOO COOL, SIR! LOOK! YOU DATE BACK TO THE MIDDLE JURASSIC!

YES, BUT YOUR HEAD IS IN THE CRETACEOUS.

GIGANTORAPTOR

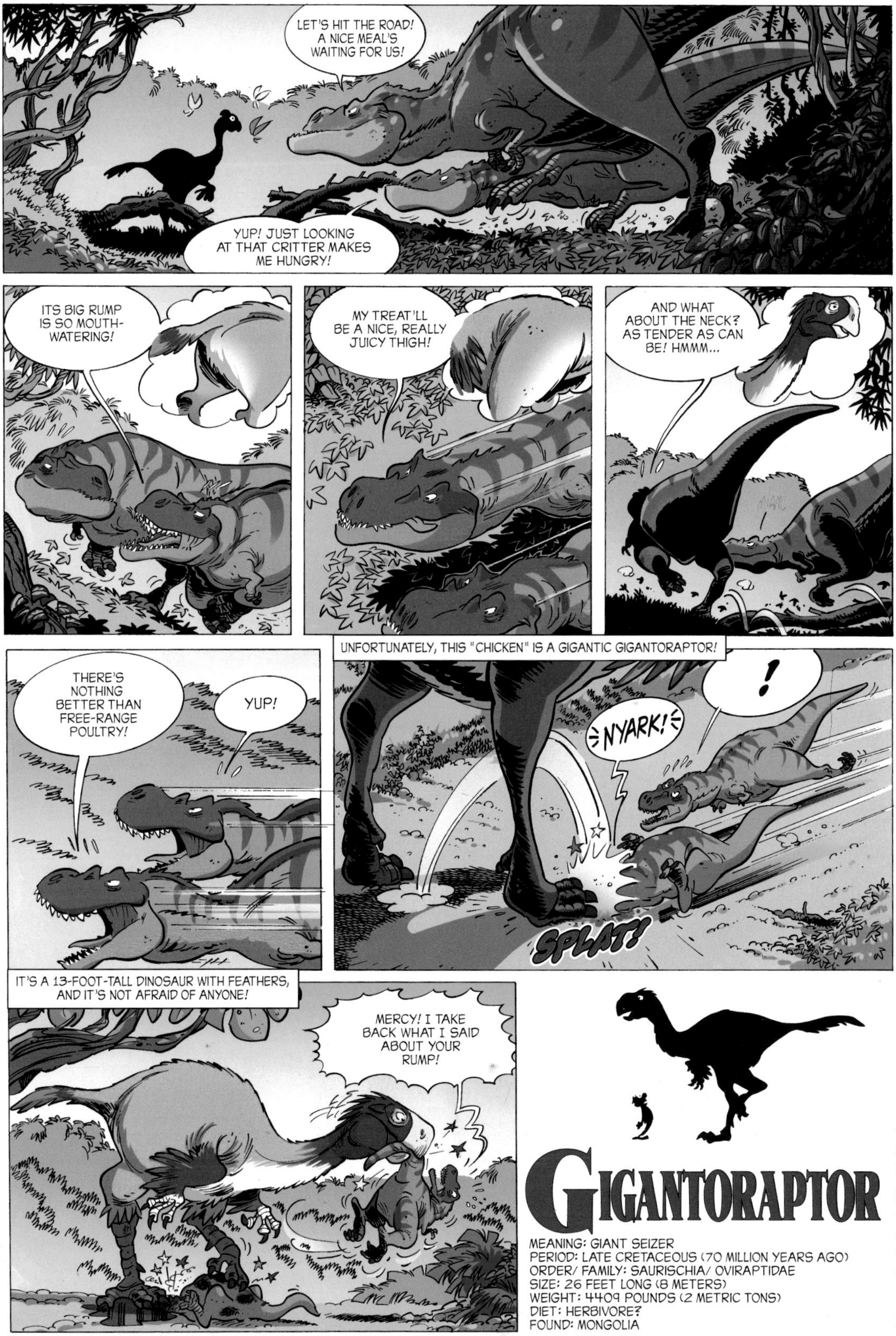
LET'S HIT THE ROAD! A NICE MEAL'S WAITING FOR US!
YUP! JUST LOOKING AT THAT CRITTER MAKES ME HUNGRY!
ITS BIG RUMP IS SO MOUTH-WATERING!
MY TREAT'LL BE A NICE, REALLY JUICY THIGH!
AND WHAT ABOUT THE NECK? AS TENDER AS CAN BE! HMMM...
THERE'S NOTHING BETTER THAN FREE-RANGE POULTRY!
YUP!
UNFORTUNATELY, THIS "CHICKEN" IS A GIGANTIC GIGANTORAPTOR!
!
NYARK!
SPLAT!
IT'S A 13-FOOT-TALL DINOSAUR WITH FEATHERS, AND IT'S NOT AFRAID OF ANYONE!
MERCY! I TAKE BACK WHAT I SAID ABOUT YOUR RUMP!

GIGANTORAPTOR

MEANING: GIANT SEIZER
PERIOD: LATE CRETACEOUS (70 MILLION YEARS AGO)
ORDER/ FAMILY: SAURISCHIA/ OVIRAPTIDAE
SIZE: 26 FEET LONG (8 METERS)
WEIGHT: 4409 POUNDS (2 METRIC TONS)
DIET: HERBIVORE?
FOUND: MONGOLIA

ARNAUTOSAURUS & GIGANTOBLOZ

THE FOOD CHAIN

TAKE ANY OLD HERBIVORE... EDMONTOSAURUS, FOR EXAMPLE.

THESE LEAVES SURE TASTE FUNNY...

CHOMP CHOMP

¿COUGH COUGH?

?

YOU CAN'T MAKE IT EAT MEAT!

YUCK!

CAN'T WE TAKE A PEACEFUL SIESTA IN THE BUSHES ANYMORE?

!

AND TAKE ANY OLD CARNIVORE. FOR EXAMPLE, TROODON...

UMM... YOU WANT MY BRANCH, RIGHT?

TAKE A LITTLE GUESS ABOUT WHAT THEY EAT...

WE ONLY EAT MEAT LIKE YOU, SAUSAGE!

¡EEEEEK!

IT'S ONE OF NATURE'S LAWS: IN ORDER TO SURVIVE, LIVING BEINGS EAT OTHERS IN A PRECISE ORDER. THIS IS THE "FOOD CHAIN."

EAT

EAT

THE T. REX HAS ITS OWN IDEA ABOUT THE FOOD CHAIN...

COME ON, FOOD! FORM A CHAIN. IT'LL BE QUICKER FOR GULPING YOU DOWN!

@#£*% NATURE! WHY AREN'T I AT THE TOP OF THE CHAIN?

SCUTELLOSAURUS

EEERK! >OW!<

CRACK

I'M FED UP WITH BEING MUNCHED ON! I'M NOT FOOD!

BAH, FOR ME YOU'RE JUST A SNACK...

...A NOISY ONE!

WHICH IS WHY THE BODY OF THE SCUTELLOSAURUS EVOLVED TO PROTECT ITSELF...

NOT BAD, THIS NEW SCALE ARMOR!

IT'S ONE OF THE VERY FIRST "THYREOPHORA," A GROUP OF ARMORED DINOSAURS...

>PHHHTTT!<

DID YA HEAR THAT, UGLY?

...THAT WOULD BE JOINED LATER ON BY THE FAMOUS STEGOSAURUS AND ANKYLOSAURUS.

AT LEAST WE--

--ARE EQUIPPED TO DEFEND OURSELVES!

AND, NO, THE SCUTELLOSAURUS HAD NOTHING TO DEFEND ITSELF WITH.

IN THE MEANTIME, I FEEL LESS PAIN. THAT'S ALREADY SOMETHING.

GRACK! CRACK!

SCUTELLOSAURUS

MEANING: LITTLE-SHIELDED LIZARD
PERIOD: EARLY JURASSIC (190-200 MILLION YEARS AGO)
ORDER/ FAMILY: ORNITHISCHIA/ THYREOPHORA
SIZE: 4 FEET LONG (1.2 METERS)
WEIGHT: 22 POUNDS (10 KG)
DIET: HERBIVORE
FOUND: UNITED STATES (ARIZONA)

PLUMERI & BROZ

MOSASAURUS

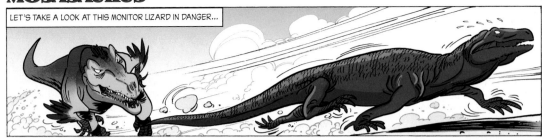

LET'S TAKE A LOOK AT THIS MONITOR LIZARD IN DANGER...

I'LL GET MY REVENGE, YOU DIRTY DINOSAUR!

?

SOME SCIENTISTS THINK IT WAS SO WELL ADAPTED TO MARINE LIFE...

I KNOW I'LL ENJOY IT HERE!

...THAT MILLIONS OF YEARS LATER IT BECAME THE TERRIBLE...

MOSASAURUS! RED ALERT!

I'M GETTING MY REVENGE ON THOSE DINOSAURS...

...MOSASAURUS. ONE OF THE BIGGEST PREDATORS OF ITS TIME!

VENGEANCE!

SOMETIMES SPECIES EVOLVE SURPRISINGLY!

¡ARGH!¿ COME HELP ME! WHERE'RE YOU GOING?

GIVE ME SEVERAL MILLION YEARS TO BECOME A GREAT BIG HULK, TOO!

MOSASAURUS

MEANING: MEUSE RIVER LIZARD
PERIOD: LATE CRETACEOUS (65-70 MILLION YEARS AGO)
ORDER/ FAMILY: SQUAMATA/ MOSAURIDAE
SIZE: 59 FEET LONG (18 METERS)
WEIGHT: 16.5 TONS (15 METRIC TONS)
DIET: PISCIVORE
FOUND: THE WHOLE WORLD

EGGS

WE KNOW QUITE A FEW THINGS ABOUT DINOSAUR EGGS...

SO DO YOU KNOW HOW TO CRACK THEIR BIG SHELLS?

>OUCH<

CRACK

SINOSAUROPTERYX EGGS WERE MUCH SMALLER THAN CHICKENS' EGGS.

>CLUCK CLUCK<

SO SMALL AND CUTE!

CHICKEN* SINOSAU-ROPTERYX

THOSE OF A TROODON WERE GOOD-SIZED.

THERE NEEDS TO BE ROOM FOR OUR SUPER BRAINS!

TAP TAP

CHICKEN TROODON

AND SAUROPOD EGGS LOOKED LIKE SOCCER BALLS.

IF YOU DO THAT, I'LL EAT YOU PERSONALLY!

CHICKEN SAUROPOD

MOST THEROPODS LAID EGGS THAT WERE STRETCHED OUT.

>NYEE NYEE<

IT'S YOUR EGGS THAT WERE STRETCHED OUT, NOT YOU!

CHICKEN THEROPOD

WE ALSO KNOW THAT OVIRAPTORS PUT THEIR EGGS IN A CIRCLE TO INCUBATE THEM.

>RAAH...< GOTTA GRAB THESE EGGS...

OK, BAD IDEA...

CHICKEN OVIRAPTOR

WE RECENTLY DISCOVERED AN EXCEPTIONAL EGG...

THE SUPER-OMELET IS MINE!

...1.3 FEET LONG AND 6 INCHES (40 CM LONG AND 15 CM) WIDE!

ARE YOU CRAZY!? THAT'D REALLY HURT!

WELL, THEN? IS THAT EGG COMING?

I REFUSE TO LAY SOMETHING LIKE THAT!

CHICKEN GIANT EGG

PLUMERI & BLOZ

MASSOSPONDYLUS

THE OLDEST DINOSAUR NEST DISCOVERED DATES BACK TO 200 MILLION YEARS AGO!

ITS OWNER, THE MASSOSPONDYLUS, TOOK ESPECIALLY GOOD CARE OF ITS EGGS.

NOW YOU'RE NICELY ARRANGED, MY DARLINGS!

CLEAR OUT OF HERE, MAMMALS!

BUT, OF COURSE, THESE NESTS CREATED SO MUCH GREED...

LEAVE MY EGGS ALONE!

BLAM

DON'T YOU DARE!

SHAKE A LEG! IT SAW US!

...FROM CARNIVOROUS DINOSAURS, TOO.

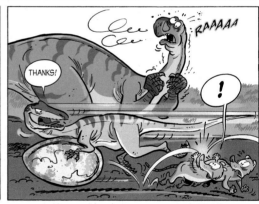

RAAAAA

THANKS!

!

:RAAAH!:

LEAVE MY EGGS IN PEACE!

THAT MASSOSPONDYLUS IS NUTS!

AND WE'RE SURPRISED THE DINOSAURS DISAPPEARED!

MASSOSPONDYLUS

MEANING: LONGER VERTEBRAE
PERIOD: EARLY JURASSIC (183-200 MILLION YEARS AGO)
ORDER/ FAMILY: SAURISCHIA/ MASSOSPONDYDAE
SIZE: 13 FEET LONG (4 METERS)
WEIGHT: 441 POUNDS (200 KILOGRAMS)
DIET: HERBIVORE
FOUND: SOUTH AFRICA, LESOTHO, UNITED STATES (?)

BEFORE THE DINOSAURS

DINOSAURS APPEARED 250 MILLION YEARS AGO.

BUT BEFORE THE DINOSAURS, WHAT WAS THERE ON THE EARTH?

FOLLOW ME! THAT'S WHAT WE'RE ABOUT TO DISCOVER!

BEFORE THE DINOSAURS, THERE WAS NOTHING...

THAT'S CLEVER. WE WENT BACK TOO FAR.

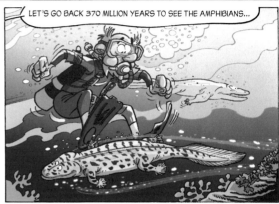

LET'S GO BACK 370 MILLION YEARS TO SEE THE AMPHIBIANS...

...WHO DISCOVERED DRY LAND, DEVELOPED LUNGS TO BREATHE...

IT'S WEIRD HERE.

...AND LEGS FOR MOVING FORWARD.

I'M SURE YOU TASTE GOOD, THINGAMAJIG!

THEY'RE WHERE REPTILES CAME FROM, 315 MILLION YEARS AGO.

THEIR INVENTION FOR SURVIVING WAS LAYING SOLID EGGS.

HEY! GIVE JUNIOR BACK!

OVER THE COURSE OF TIME, THESE REPTILES TOOK ON VERY DIVERSE FORMS...

WITH BLASTED JAWS!

OOUUCH!

SOME REPTILES EQUIPPED THEMSELVES WITH A SHELL...

LIKE TORTOISES!

GET OFF MY BACK!

OTHERS BECAME PERFECT CRAWLERS...

HE'S RUNNING FOR HIS LIFE!

HE'S LUCKY!

...OR EVOLVED INTO MAMMAL-LIKE REPTILES.

THESE ARE THE ANCESTORS OF MAMMALS!

CALL ME, DADDY, THEN.

BUT THE ARCHOSAUR GROUP DOMINATED.

THIS GROUP CONTAINS CROCODILES, PTEROSAURS, AND DINOSAURS.

THEY BENEFITED FROM THE DISAPPEARANCE OF NUMEROUS SPECIES DUE TO CATASTROPHES...

WE HAVE SOME DOUBTS ABOUT THIS, BUT WE THINK THEY MIGHT HAVE BEEN CAUSED BY SUPER VOLCANOES...

...OR GIANT METEORITES THAT CRASHED INTO THE EARTH.

QUICK, MY HELMET!

SEVENTY PERCENT OF TERRESTRIAL SPECIES THUS DISAPPEARED, LEAVING THE FIELD FREE FOR DINOSAURS!

WHAT FOOLS! THAT WON'T HAPPEN TO DINOSAURS!

BETTER NOT TELL THEM WHAT'S WAITING FOR THEM!

MAJUNGASAURUS

MAJUNGASAURUS

MEANING: MAHAJANGA (PROVINCE OF MADAGASCAR) LIZARD
PERIOD: LATE CRETACEOUS (65-70 MILLION YEARS AGO)
ORDER/ FAMILY: SAURISCHIA/ ABELISAURIDAE
SIZE: 30 FEET LONG (9 METERS)
WEIGHT: 2205 POUNDS (1 METRIC TON)
DIET: CARNIVORE
FOUND: MADAGASCAR

COULD DINOSAURS SWIM?

IF WE TOSS A CAT INTO A BATHTUB...

IT MANAGES TO SWIM!

HSSS!

SO WHY COULDN'T A DINOSAUR SWIM?

WE ALREADY KNOW THAT DINOSAURS WENT INTO THE WATER...

I'VE INVENTED A NEW SWIMMING STROKE!

SINCE WE FOUND CLAW TRACKS AT THE BOTTOM OF A RIVER!

THE BOUNCING BREASTSTROKE! HOP! HOP!

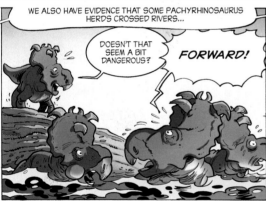

WE ALSO HAVE EVIDENCE THAT SOME PACHYRHINOSAURUS HERDS CROSSED RIVERS...

DOESN'T THAT SEEM A BIT DANGEROUS?

FORWARD!

SINCE WE FOUND FOSSILS OF A FEW UNLUCKY ONES THAT DROWNED...

≴GLUB GLUB≴

TRY TO KEEP UP WITH EVERYONE!

A LIGHT DINOSAUR LIKE COMPSOGNATHUS WOULD HAVE ALL IT NEEDED TO BE A GOOD SWIMMER...

COME ON IN AND SWIM. THE WATER'S GREAT!

BUT FOR BRACHIOSAURUS, IT WOULD SEEM A BIT LESS CLEAR...

SWIM? FIND ME A PLACE WHERE I WON'T HIT BOTTOM...

!

SMARTY PANTS!

SAURONIOPS

DO YOU KNOW THE *LORD OF THE RINGS?* SOME PALEONTOLOGISTS ARE FANS OF IT...

GREAT MOVIE!

AS GOOD AS THE BOOK!

THE LORD OF THE RINGS

ESPECIALLY OF EVIL SAURON, THE EYE THAT SEES EVERYTHING...

I SEE YOU!

THEY PAID HIM HOMAGE BY NAMING A NEW DINOSAUR AFTER HIM...

DID YOU SEE THE UGLY BUMP IT HAS UNDER ITS EYE?

WE'LL JUST HAVE TO CALL IT "SAURONIOPS"...

THE EYE OF SAURON!

ACTUALLY, SAURONIOPS WOULD HAVE BEEN TERRIFYING.

I SEE YOU!

MY PRECIOUS...

I SAW YOU! YOU STOLE MY EGG! GIVE IT BACK TO ME!

NO! NOT MY PRECIOUS!

WAIT, I'LL HELP YOU, COUSIN!

BUT IF PALEONTOLOGISTS HAD SEEN ANOTHER MOVIE?

HOP

FOR EXAMPLE...

...RATATOUILLE, THE ADVENTURES OF A RAT CHEF!

GO ON, MAKE AN OMELET!

RAAAAH! HE BROKE MY PRECIOUS!

CRACK!

SAURONIOPS

MEANING: EYE OF SAURON
PERIOD: LATE CRETACEOUS (93-99 MILLION YEARS AGO)
ORDER/ FAMILY: SAURISCHIA/ CHARCHARODONTOSAURIDAE
SIZE: 39 FEET LONG (12 METERS)
WEIGHT: 6.6 TONS? (6 METRIC TONS?)
DIET: CARNIVORE
FOUND: NORTH AFRICA (MOROCCO)

PLUMERI-&-BLOZ

FIGHTS BETWEEN GIANT HERBIVORES INEVITABLY WOULD'VE LEFT MARKS!

CORYTHOSAURUS

MEANING: HELMET LIZARD
PERIOD: LATE CRETACEOUS (75 MILLION YEARS AGO)
ORDER/ FAMILY: ORNITHISCHIA/ HADROSAURIDAE
SIZE: 30 FEET LONG (9 METERS)
WEIGHT: 4 TONS (4 METRIC TONS)
DIET: HERBIVORE
FOUND: CANADA, UNITED STATES

CHICKENOSAURUS

WHAT DO YOU THINK? WHICH OF TODAY'S ANIMALS IS CLOSEST TO T. REX?

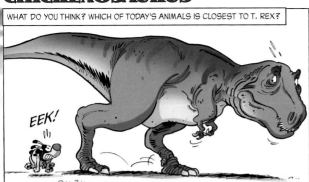

EEK!

ACCORDING TO SCIENTISTS, THE CHICKEN!

WOOF! WOOF!

THIS LITTLE THINGIE HERE?

:CLUCK?:

THAT THEORY PUSHED THEM TO DO EXPERIMENTS ON CHICKEN EMBRYOS.

COME ON! THE FIRST ONE TO TRANSFORM ITSELF WILL GET A STEAK!

THE RESULT? THEY MANAGED TO GROW A LONG TAIL ON A "CHICKENOSAURUS..."

:CLUCK!: I'LL SHOW YOU!

:WOOF!: THE DAY YOU SCARE ME, CHICKEN WILL HAVE TEETH!

EXACTLY! THEY ALSO GOT THEM TO GROW TEETH AND LEGS WITH CLAWS!

YIKES! YIKES!

WHICH CONFIRMS THAT THESE BIRDS ARE THE DINOSAURS' DESCENDANTS!

ROOOAR!

I'D SAY IT AGAIN, LOUDER. :CLUCK!:

UM, ROAR.

WE CAN ONLY HOPE WE'LL NEVER SEE A SCENE LIKE THIS ONE!

NICE. A STEAK!

BIG EATERS

THE UNITED STATES WAS FULL OF HUGE EATERS 150 MILLION YEARS AGO.

APATASAURS, THAT WAY!

DIPLODOCUS, WAIT TWO MINUTES BEFORE PASSING THROUGH!

BRACHIOSAURS, DON'T FORGET TO ONLY TAKE THINGS THAT ARE HIGH UP!

OF COURSE. STOP STRESSING OUT.

SAUROPODS: THEY'RE JUST A LOT OF WORRY AND ORGANIZATION...

THEY EAT 1,102 POUNDS OF VEGETATION A DAY. AS A RESULT, YOU NEED TO TELL THEM WHERE THEY CAN HELP THEMSELVES.

WE THINK THAT DINOSAURS FED AT DIFFERENT HEIGHTS, ALLOWING THE VEGETATION TO HOLD OUT.

BOSS! BOSS!

DID YOU SEE? YOUR SYSTEM OF ORGANIZATION ROCKS!

WELL, EXACTLY...

WE FORGOT BARBOSAURUS AND CAMARASAURUS...

NOT TO MENTION SUPERSAURUS!

DID THESE DINOSAURS DISAPPEAR "QUICKLY" DUE TO A LACK OF FOOD? IT'S POSSIBLE!

SCIPIONYX

THIS BABY SCIPIONYX, NICKNAMED "CIRO," IS A STAR...

IT'S THE FIRST DINOSAUR EVER FOUND IN ITALY...A COMPLETE FOSSIL!

THIS DINOSAUR HAD A FLEETING LIFE: IT ONLY LIVED A FEW HOURS!

EXAMINING ITS INTESTINES SHOWS THAT IT ATE ITALIAN CUISINE...

SUCH A NICE DINOSAUR ONLY MADE ITALIAN PALEONTOLOGISTS WANT MORE...

UNFORTUNATELY, ITALIAN DINOSAURS ARE STILL RARE...

BUT THE ITALIAN SOIL IS RICH WITH OTHER COMPENSATIONS!

SCIPIONYX

MEANING: SCIPIO'S CLAW
PERIOD: EARLY CRETACEOUS (113 MILLION YEARS AGO)
ORDER/ FAMILY: SAURISCHIA/ COMPSOGNATHIDAE
SIZE: 1.5 FEET LONG (45 CENTIMETERS) (BABY)/
7 FEET LONG (2 METERS) (ADULT)
WEIGHT: 11 OUNCES (300 GRAMS) (BABY)/
88 POUNDS (40 KG) (ADULT)
DIET: CARNIVORE, PISCIVORE
FOUND: ITALY

YOUR ATTENTION, PLEASE! HERE COMES KING GUANLONG I!

? ? CRUNCH CRUNCH...

I SAID, "HERE COMES KING GUANLONG I!

SEE ME!

HAH! HAH! WHAT A JOKE!

SPLOTCH

HEY, MY NAME MEANS "CROWNED DRAGON!" I'M THE FIRST OF THE TYRANNOSAURS!

NONSENSE!

WHAT'S THIS LACK OF RESPECT?

WHY SHOULD YOU BE THE KING?

YOU'RE NOT EVEN THE BIGGEST DINOSAUR AROUND...

AND THE OTHER CARNIVORES CAN BEAT YOU TO A PULP!

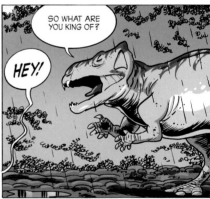

SO WHAT ARE YOU KING OF?

HEY!

HELP!

I... I'M SINKING!

AH, WELL, NOW IT'S CLEAR. YOU'RE THE KING OF FOOLS!

AND YES, THE GUANLONG DISCOVERED DIED FOOLISHLY TRAPPED IN THE MUD!

GUANLONG

MEANING: CROWNED DRAGON
PERIOD: LATE JURASSIC (160 MILLION YEARS AGO)
ORDER/ FAMILY: SAURISCHIA/ PROCERATOSAURIDAE
SIZE: 10 FEET LONG (3 METERS)
WEIGHT: 198 POUNDS (90 KG)
DIET: CARNIVORE
FOUND: CHINA

ALMOST EVERYTHING ABOUT T. REX?

DINOSAUR TALES

BEELZEBUFO

MEANING: DEVIL TOAD
PERIOD: LATE CRETACEOUS (70 MILLION YEARS AGO)
ORDER/ FAMILY: ANURA/ LEPTOYLIDAE
SIZE: 16 INCHES LONG (40 CM)
WEIGHT: 9 POUNDS (4 KG)
DIET: CARNIVORE
FOUND: MADAGASCAR

CAL ORCKO

CAL ORCKO'S SITE IN BOLIVIA IS AMAZING...

THEY'VE FOUND 5,000 PRINTS FROM AT LEAST 8 DIFFERENT SPECIES OF DINOSAURS THERE!

THE TRACKS ARE ON STEEP TERRAIN, WHICH ROSE UP OVER TIME...

SINCE IT WAS A COMPLETELY FLAT DINOSAUR HIGHWAY 70 MILLION YEARS AGO!

THE ROAD WAS TRAVELED BY SOME THEROPODS (CARNIVORES) AND ARMORED DINOSAURS...

SO ARE YOU GOING TO GET MOVING, GRAMPS?!

I MAY NOT GO FAST, BUT I'M IN FRONT OF YOU!

BY ORNITHOPODS (SMALL HERBIVORES) AND TITANOSAURS (LONG-NECK, ARMORED DINOSAURS).

I'M FED UP WITH THESE HEAVY FEET THAT HIDE THE WAY!

AT LEAST YOU'RE WALKING N THE SHADE!

AH... WELL, WE'VE REACHED THE TOLL BOOTH!

GULP!

WITHOUT FORGETTING ABOUT THE PRESENCE OF GIANT CARNIVORES!

FANK YOU! SEE YOU SOON!

THEY RAISED THE TOLL AGAIN!

YUP, WE GOT HIT HARD!

BIG AMERICAN NAMES

A NUMBER OF AMERICAN PALEONTOLOGISTS HAVE REALLY HELPED US KNOW DINOSAURS BETTER...

JACK HORNER, AMONG OTHERS, SHOWED THAT DINOSAURS TAKE CARE OF THEIR YOUNG.

HERE'S THE MAIASAURA MATERNITY WARD...

HEY! ONLY AUTHORIZED PERSONNEL ARE ALLOWED TO ENTER!

HE WAS A CONSULTANT FOR *JURASSIC PARK*...

THE CHARACTER OF ALAN GRANT WAS INSPIRED BY YOU.

BUT I'M A LOT BETTER LOOKING!

AS WELL AS ROBERT BAKKER, WHO SAID, LONG BEFORE ANYONE ELSE...

SOME DINOSAURS HAD FEATHERS. YOU'LL HAVE TO GET USED TO IT.

FINALLY SOMEONE WHO KNOWS US!

PAUL SERENO DISCOVERED AFRICAN DINOSAURS, LIKE THE MONSTROUS CARCHARODONTOSAURUS.

FOUND YOU!

⇥ROOOH!⇤ YOU'RE TOO GOOD! IT'S YOUR TURN TO HIDE.

WHEN HE WAS LITTLE, THOMAS HOLTZ ALWAYS SAID...

WHEN I GROW UP, I'M GOING TO BE A T. REX!

WHY, YES. THAT'S NICE.

TODAY HE KNOWS TYRANNOSAURS BETTER THAN ANYONE.

YEEHAW!

HOW'D I GET INTO THIS?

WITH EXPERTS LIKE THESE, YOUNG PALEONTOLOGISTS...

HOW ABOUT IF I BECOME A T. REX EXPERT?

ALREADY TAKEN!

AND FEATHERED DINOSAURS?

ALREADY TAKEN, TOO!

PALEONTOLOGIST CONVENTION

SO WHAT'S LEFT, THEN?

...FACE TOUGH COMPETITION TO FIND THEIR NICHE.

STUDYING COPROLITES...

DINOSAUR POOP!

34

WE DASPLETOSAURS HAVE TOO MUCH TO DO WITH ALL HESE HORNED DINOSAURS...

QUITE NORMAL, AS IT'S THE ANCESTOR OF T. REX.

WE CAN PLAY HIDE AND SEEK...

ROAR

HAVE FUN WITH THE FASTEST RUNNERS...

AND IT'S LOTS OF FUN TO POP THEIR TOPS!

PLOP

CRACK

ON THE OTHER HAND, SPEAKING OF GAMES...

THEIRS ARE TRULY DUMB!

YEOW!

15-0!

DASPLETOSAURUS

MEANING: FRIGHTFUL LIZARD
PERIOD: LATE CRETACEOUS (72-80 MILLION YEARS AGO)
ORDER/ FAMILY: SAURISCHIA/ TYRANNOSAURIDAE
SIZE: 30 FEET LONG (9 METERS)
WEIGHT: 4 TONS (4 METRIC TONS)
DIET: CARNIVORE
FOUND: UNITED STATES (MONTANA) AND CANADA (ALBERTA)

PLUMERI & BAO

STYRACOSAURUS

MEANING: SPIKED LIZARD
PERIOD: LATE CRETACEOUS (72-80 MILLION YEARS AGO)
ORDER/ FAMILY: ORNITHISCHIA/ CERTAPSIA
SIZE: 16 FEET LONG (5 METERS)
WEIGHT: 6614 POUNDS (3 METRIC TONS)
DIET: HERBIVORE
FOUND: UNITED STATES, CANADA

LYTHRONAX

THE DISCOVERY OF A GREAT-UNCLE OF T. REX IN 2013 CAUSED A SENSATION...

HERE'S THE TERRIFYING LYTHRONAX, WHOSE NAME MEANS "GORE KING!"

GRAAOOR

THE TERRIBLE DIABLOCERATOPS ("HORNED-FACE DEVIL") ALSO LIVED IN THE SAME ERA.

SNORT!

IN THIS HELL ON EARTH, ONLY THE NASTIEST COULD SURVIVE!

ROOAR!

BRAOO

HELLO, SWEETIES!

EH? WHO THE HECK'RE YOU?

;SMACK!; YOU ARE TOO CUTE!

WHO AM I? I'M A FRIEND OF THE PLANTS AND THE SUN!

OH, HELLO, LITTLE DRAGONFLY!

CRUNCH

WE'VE NEVER FOUND TRACKS OF THIS LITTLE DINOSAUR, UNLIKE THOSE OF THE LYTHRONAX!

CHOMP

IT'S NOT A BIG LOSS.

LYTHRONAX

MEANING: GORE KING
PERIOD: LATE CRETACEOUS (80 MILLION YEARS AGO)
ORDER/ FAMILY: SAURISCHIA/ TYRANNOSAURIDAE
SIZE: 26 FEET LONG (8 METERS)
WEIGHT: 5512 POUNDS (2.5 METRIC TONS)
DIET: CARNIVORE
FOUND: UNITED STATES (UTAH)

PLUMERI & BioZ

ATTENTION! THE FOLLOWING SCENES ARE NOT FOR THE FAINT OF HEART!

AN EOCARCHARIA LAUNCHES A SURPRISE ATTACK ON A NIGERSAURUS.

ROOAAR!

?

¡AARGGHH!!

YOUR HEAD MAKES ME WANT TO GO ON A DIET!

BOY, IS IT UGLY!

HERE'S A BIZARRE DINOSAUR WITH A JAW AS WIDE AS ITS SKULL!

I LIKE MYSELF FINE.

HEY! GO GRAZE SOMEWHERE ELSE! YOU'RE SCARING THE KIDS!

?

¿PHOOEY¿... THEY'RE EXAGGERATING A BIT THERE.

ALL THESE EMOTIONS ARE MAKING ME THIRSTY.

?!

HELP! THERE'S AN AWFUL DINOSAUR IN THE LAKE!

BOY, IS IT UGLY!

NIGERSAURUS

MEANING: NIGER REPTILE
PERIOD: EARLY JURASSIC (110-118 MILLION YEARS AGO)
ORDER/ FAMILY: SAURISCHIA/ REBBACHISAURIDAE
SIZE: 49 FEET LONG (15 METERS)
WEIGHT: 4 TONS (4 METRIC TONS)
DIET: HERBIVORE
FOUND: AFRICA (NIGER)

COMPSO'S REVENGE

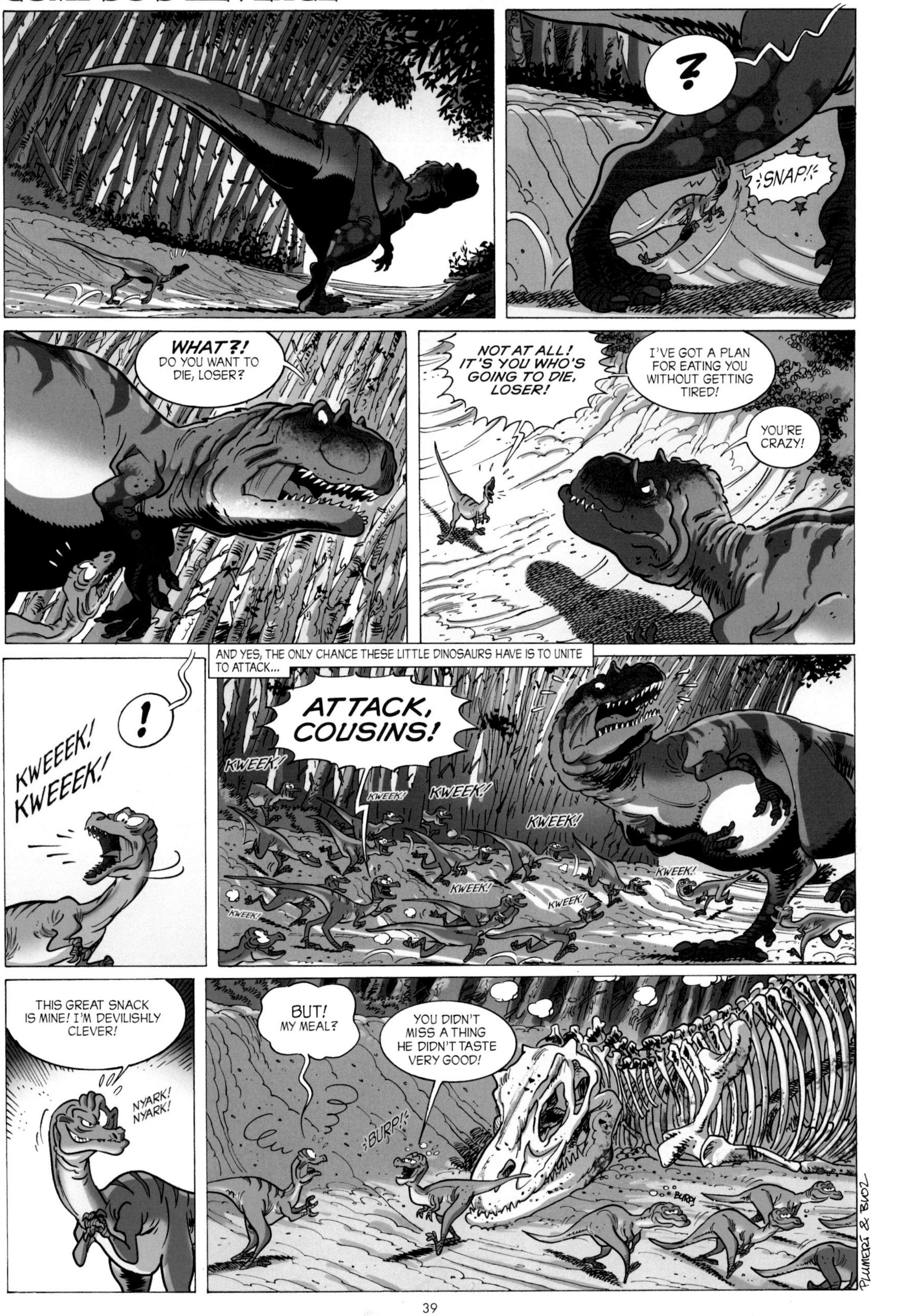

?
SNAP!
WHAT?! DO YOU WANT TO DIE, LOSER?
NOT AT ALL! IT'S YOU WHO'S GOING TO DIE, LOSER!
I'VE GOT A PLAN FOR EATING YOU WITHOUT GETTING TIRED!
YOU'RE CRAZY!
!
KWEEEK! KWEEEK!
AND YES, THE ONLY CHANCE THESE LITTLE DINOSAURS HAVE IS TO UNITE TO ATTACK...
ATTACK, COUSINS!
KWEEK!
KWEEK!
KWEEK!
KWEEK!
KWEEK!
KWEEK!
KWEEK!
KWEEK!
THIS GREAT SNACK IS MINE! I'M DEVILISHLY CLEVER!
NYARK! NYARK!
BUT! MY MEAL?
YOU DIDN'T MISS A THING HE DIDN'T TASTE VERY GOOD!
BURP!
BURP!
PLUMERI & BLOZ

NOT SO FAR AWAY...

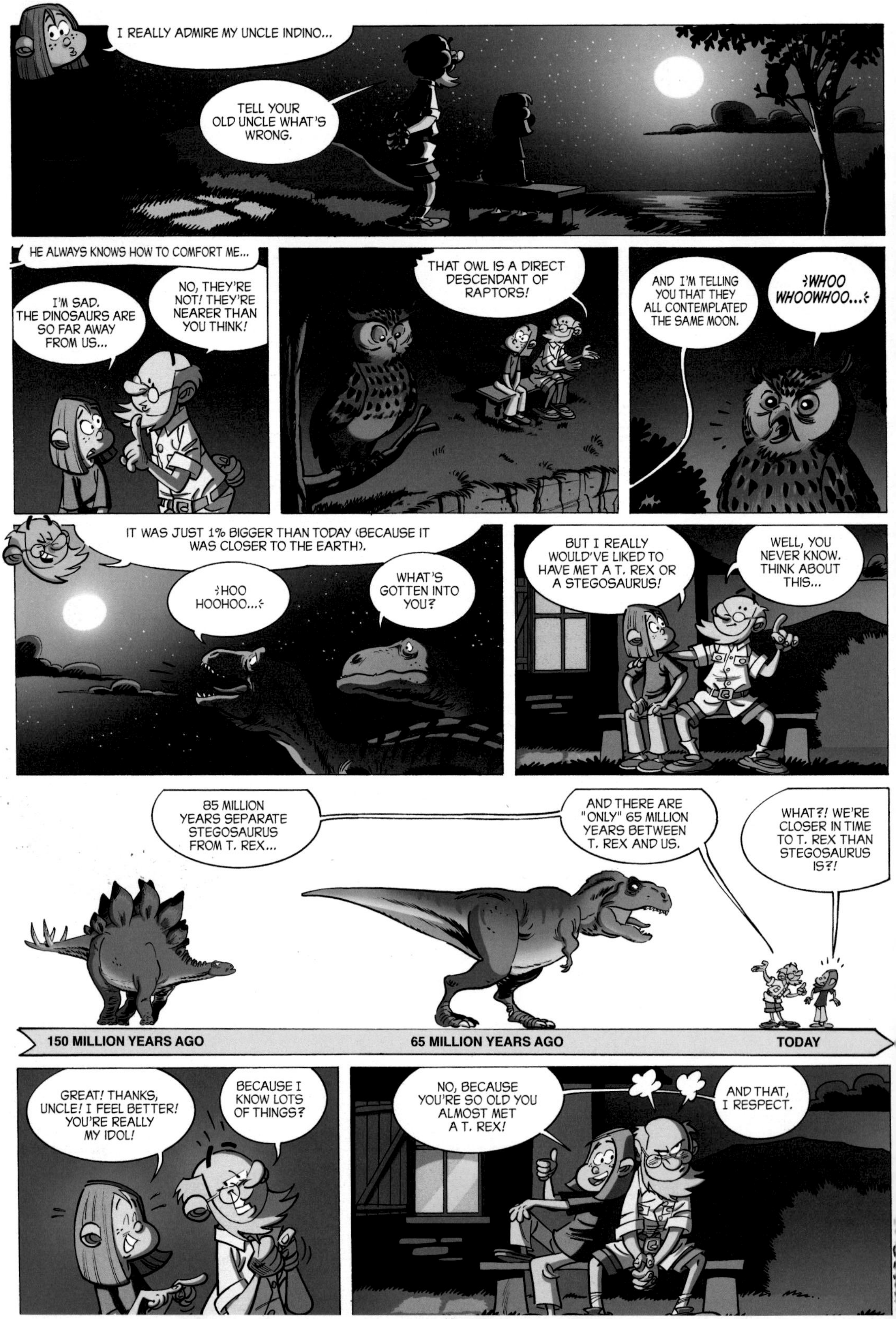

I REALLY ADMIRE MY UNCLE INDINO...
TELL YOUR OLD UNCLE WHAT'S WRONG.
HE ALWAYS KNOWS HOW TO COMFORT ME...
I'M SAD. THE DINOSAURS ARE SO FAR AWAY FROM US...
NO, THEY'RE NOT! THEY'RE NEARER THAN YOU THINK!
THAT OWL IS A DIRECT DESCENDANT OF RAPTORS!
AND I'M TELLING YOU THAT THEY ALL CONTEMPLATED THE SAME MOON.
WHOO WHOOWHOO...
IT WAS JUST 1% BIGGER THAN TODAY (BECAUSE IT WAS CLOSER TO THE EARTH).
HOO HOOHOO...
WHAT'S GOTTEN INTO YOU?
BUT I REALLY WOULD'VE LIKED TO HAVE MET A T. REX OR A STEGOSAURUS!
WELL, YOU NEVER KNOW. THINK ABOUT THIS...
85 MILLION YEARS SEPARATE STEGOSAURUS FROM T. REX...
AND THERE ARE "ONLY" 65 MILLION YEARS BETWEEN T. REX AND US.
WHAT?! WE'RE CLOSER IN TIME TO T. REX THAN STEGOSAURUS IS?!
150 MILLION YEARS AGO
65 MILLION YEARS AGO
TODAY
GREAT! THANKS, UNCLE! I FEEL BETTER! YOU'RE REALLY MY IDOL!
BECAUSE I KNOW LOTS OF THINGS?
NO, BECAUSE YOU'RE SO OLD YOU ALMOST MET A T. REX!
AND THAT, I RESPECT.

Utah countryside
© Raymond M. Alf Museum of Paleontology

DISCOVERING AN AMAZING PARASAUROLOPHUS !

For Paleontologists, some discoveries are more thrilling than others. In 2009 in Utah (United States), a nearly complete fossil of a magnificent duck-billed dinosaur was found: a Parasaurolophus...barely a year old! Let's go meet the dinosaur they named, "Joe"...

THE DISCOVERY

Southern Utah, U.S. The story of a discovery unlike any other begins in this magnificent countryside, at times steep and at times covered with prairies and forests. Directed by paleontologists Don Lofgren and Andy Farke of the Raymond M. Alf Museum of Paleontology, students regularly examine the rocks, looking for traces of ancient inhabitants.

One fateful day in August, 2009, three students—Kevin Terris, Cameron Lutz, and Christian Quick—and their professor, Andy Farke, leave to lead excavations in the direction of an as yet unexplored hill. Along the way, Kevin Terris spots something inlaid in the rock. According to Andy, it's a fragment of a dinosaur rib not worth wasting much time over. That type of bone is common in the area; digging it out would take a lot of time. And since the region has already been explored, there is little chance of finding anything else.

Andy Farke continues along the path, walking to the other side of the rock and notices a little pebble. He picks it up and, lo and behold: a fossilized dinosaur skull appears before his eyes! The group gets interested in the rib fragment again...which proves to be the toe bones of a dinosaur! No doubt about it, there's a whole dinosaur skeleton hidden in between!

Everyone gets excited. Given the size of the bones, it's clearly a baby dinosaur. But they will have to wait until the following summer to know more and to know what species it is, because meticulously extracting a skeleton like that takes a long time.

The right side of the dinosaur's skull and neck.

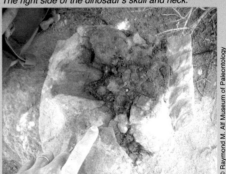

© Raymond M. Alf Museum of Paleontology

Toe and skin print of the dinosaur.

Summer 2010. The Alf Museum and The Webb Schools (a private high school) teams return to the site. The boulder that the fossil is imprisoned under is very hard. To extract it, they have to use a jackhammer, but with great care so as to avoid damaging anything. After removing as much of the rocks as possible, the skeleton is wrapped into plaster strips. The assembly weighs nearly 1,102 pounds (500 kg) and is in an inaccessible area, so there is no other way to remove it besides attaching it to a helicopter.

Kevin Terris, the student who discovered the fossil.

Removing the fossil.

PREPARING THE FOSSIL

It's at this point that fossil preparator Mike Stokes enters the scene. Grain by grain, he removes the rock around the fossil by crushing it with compressed air. He glues the most fragile bone fragments and reassembles the broken parts.

Cleaning the fossil will take him 1,300 hours of work! But everyone will be rewarded. While they originally think that the skull is incomplete, they discover that it is, in fact, nearly intact. And for paleontologists, the skull is one of the most important parts (and the rarest) because it is indispensable for thoroughly studying a dinosaur. This discovery allows them to confirm that this is a Parasaurolophus. (They thought they might have found a Gryposaurus.)

Once the fossil is prepared, the baby Parasaurolophus almost comes to life. He's named, "Joe," in honor of Joe Augustyn, a generous donor to the museum.

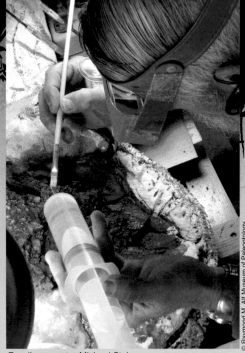

© Raymond M. Alf Museum of Paleontology

Fossil preparator Michael Stokes.

Andy Farke examines the bones.

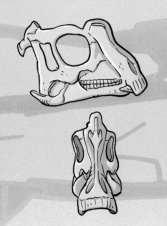

Joe's skeleton.

STUDYING THE FOSSIL

For months, a team of five researchers study the fossil in every which way, thanks to state-of-the-art techniques: it is scanned and then a 3D model is created on a computer. And here are the conclusions of their research, published in 2013.

Joe was discovered in an ancient riverbed, which allowed him to be preserved this well, as air was unable to cause the carcass to deteriorate.

The dinosaur skull lets us know more about its growth. The Parasaurolophus is well known for the crest decorating its head. The crest would have served to amplify sounds like a trumpet (useful for communicating or frightening predators). In adults, which could reach 30 feet (9 meters) in length and 6,614 pounds (3 metric tons), the crest could be as large as 7 feet long (2 meters)! Joe's skull has a lump that shows where his crest was starting to "push through."

© Raymond M. Alf Museum of Paleontology

Scanning the fossil.

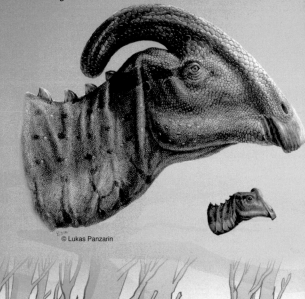

© Lukas Panzarin

By examining thin slices of bone under the microscope, the team discovered the area where the blood vessels and bone cells were. Comparing these with similar ones from species living today, scientists were able to confirm that Joe was not an adult. He would have been less than a year old and 6 feet long (1.8 meters). In short, he was a big, beautiful baby.

Bone cells viewed under a microscope.

© Scott Hartman (baby dinosaur), Matt Martyniuk (dinosaur), Andrew Farke (human)

QUESTIONS FOR ANDY FARKE

Paleontologist at the Raymond M. Alf Museum of Paleontology

Andy Farke is sort of Joe the Parasaurolophus' dad. He has studied him in every which way and remains amazed by his new family member.

How did you feel when you saw the fossil of Joe?
When I saw his skull, my heart started to beat really hard. I was so excited I started yelling! Bit by bit, as the skeleton was revealed, it got even better.

What is the most unbelievable thing about this fossil for you?
Most unbelievable for me is Joe's small size. It's not unusual to find fragments from small dinosaurs and it's common to find pieces from large dinosaurs. To find the whole skeleton of a small dinosaur is unbelievable enough. The first time I saw the specimen after it had been prepared, I was surprised to see how small it was.

What other discovery do you dream of making now?
I would love to find Joe's little brothers and sisters, and his big brothers, too. Now that we know what a "baby" Parasaurolophus looks like, I would be curious to know how it resembles an adolescent dinosaur. And how the crest would have changed as the animal grew.

© Raymond M. Alf Museum of Paleontology

THE LIFE OF THE PARASAUROLOPHUS

Joe and his fellow Parasaurolophus lived in North America 75 million years ago. These herbivores belonged to the large family of Hadrosaurs, also called "duck-billed dinosaurs" due to the shape of their "mouths." The Parasaurolophus was an occasional biped, in other words, it walked on four legs and occasionally rose onto its rear legs.

It had hundreds of small, narrow teeth that allowed it to tear vegetation as well as to chew it. It evolved in the heart plentiful tropical vegetation, crossed by numerous rive inhabited by turtles and crocodiles.

Joe probably traveled with other adult Parasaurolophu by staying in groups, they had a better chance of defendi themselves against predators such as Teratophoneus, cousin of T. rex.

THEY ALSO LIVED 75 MILLION YEARS AGO...

Daspletosaur

Euplocephalus

Corythosaurus

Troodon

Styracosaurus

WHERE CAN YOU GO TO SEE THE PARASAUROLOPHUS?

If you get a chance to travel, you can admire Joe's fossil at the Raymond M. Alf Museum of Paleontology and on the campus of The Webb Schools in Claremont, California. Joe's discoverers put together an excellent website to share their enthusiasm: www.dinosaurjoe.org.

WATCH OUT FOR PAPERCUTℤ ™

Welcome to the fine-feathered fourth DINOSAURS graphic novel by Arnaud Plumeri and Bloz from Papercutz, the far-from-extinct humans (Homo-sapiens) dedicated to publishing great graphic novels for all ages! I'm Jim Salicrup, the Editor-in-Chief and the only person in the office who hasn't seen *Jurassic World* yet, here to enlighten and possibly inform you…

First, regarding the non-existence of the Brontosaurus (see page 5), we've got an important update on that. According to a recent issue of *Scientific American*, the Brontosaurus did exist:

> It turns out the original *Apatosaurus* and *Brontosaurus* fossils appear different enough to belong to separate groups after all. "Generally, *Brontosaurus* can be distinguished from *Apatosaurus* most easily by its neck, which is higher and less wide," says lead study author Emanuel Tschopp, a vertebrate paleontologist at the New University of Lisbon in Portugal. "So although both are very massive and robust animals, *Apatosaurus* is even more extreme than *Brontosaurus*."

Chances are, as soon as this graphic novel sees print, new evidence will be uncovered to contradict the above. That's just how it is in the exciting world of paleontology! Folks are literally digging up new information all the time. With advances in technology, more things are possible than ever before. Plus all the old information is continually being re-examined to see if it still makes sense in the context of more recent discoveries. Who would've thought there would be so much to learn about creatures who walked the earth millions of years ago? New discoveries of centuries-old bones continue at a rapid pace, while I still struggle to find my pencil on my desk.

What probably fuels our perpetual fascination with dinosaurs is the fact that's these unbelievable creatures actually did exist. At Papercutz, we publish several graphic novel series about characters that are sheer fantasy, yet the dinosaurs in DINOSAURS still seem like something out of Hollywood's imagination. For example, look at the Smurfs. Are they really any more unbelievable than the Diplodocus or the Anklylosaurus? You could say that they are because the Smurfs actually speak, and dinosaurs didn't—but you never know! The next issue of *Scientific American* may reveal that dinosaurs actually spoke (or chirped)!

Speaking of THE SMURFS, there's a new Smurfs Special out called SMURFS MONSTERS and we think you may enjoy it, even though there are all sorts of crazy monsters in it, there aren't any dinosaurs in it! Take a look at the preview of "Motro, the Forest Monster," starting on the very next page, to get a better idea of what we're talking about.

Finally, somewhat sad news… we've been informed that this volume of DINOSAURS will quite possibly be the last one. I'd suggest keeping an eye on our website, Papercutz.com, to not only find any DINOSAUR updates, but to check out all the other graphic novels we publish. I suspect you'll find something there you'd like!

Thanks,

Jim

Bonus: Special excerpt from Salicrupedia…
Salicrupsaurus (Page 47)
Meaning: Big-Headed Editor
Period: Bronze Age to Modern Age (57 Years Ago)
Order/ Family: Geekasaurs/ Salicrupidae
Size: 6'2"
Weight: 250 lbs.?
Diet: Omnivore
Found: North America (If found, return to Papercutz)

STAY IN TOUCH!
EMAIL: salicrup@papercutz.com
WEB: papercutz.com
TWITTER: @papercutzgn
FACEBOOK: PAPERCUTZGRAPHICNOVELS
MAIL: Papercutz, 160 Broadway,
Suite 700, East Wing, New York, NY 10038

MOTRO, THE FOREST MONSTER

What do you want? Who are you?

My name is Fatso! I bought all these woods from the steward so I can rip everything up and have my cows graze here!

WHAT?! Cows in MY park?

Enough wasting time! Get a move on, you all! Bust all of this up for me!

Hey! Don't smurf our swing set!

Master Fatso said to smash everything!

HAW!

He's a madman!

OH! My potentillas! NO!

Cut those bushes. It's full of goblins in there!

Let me chase after those blue goblins, and I'll bring you the most beautiful oak trees that they protect!

Okay, be quick about it!

NO! You can't touch the hundred-year-old oak!

Shut up, you fat cow!

We won't let you smurf that tree!

Ha! Ha! Ha! Step aside, you puny shrimp!

© Peyo

2

49

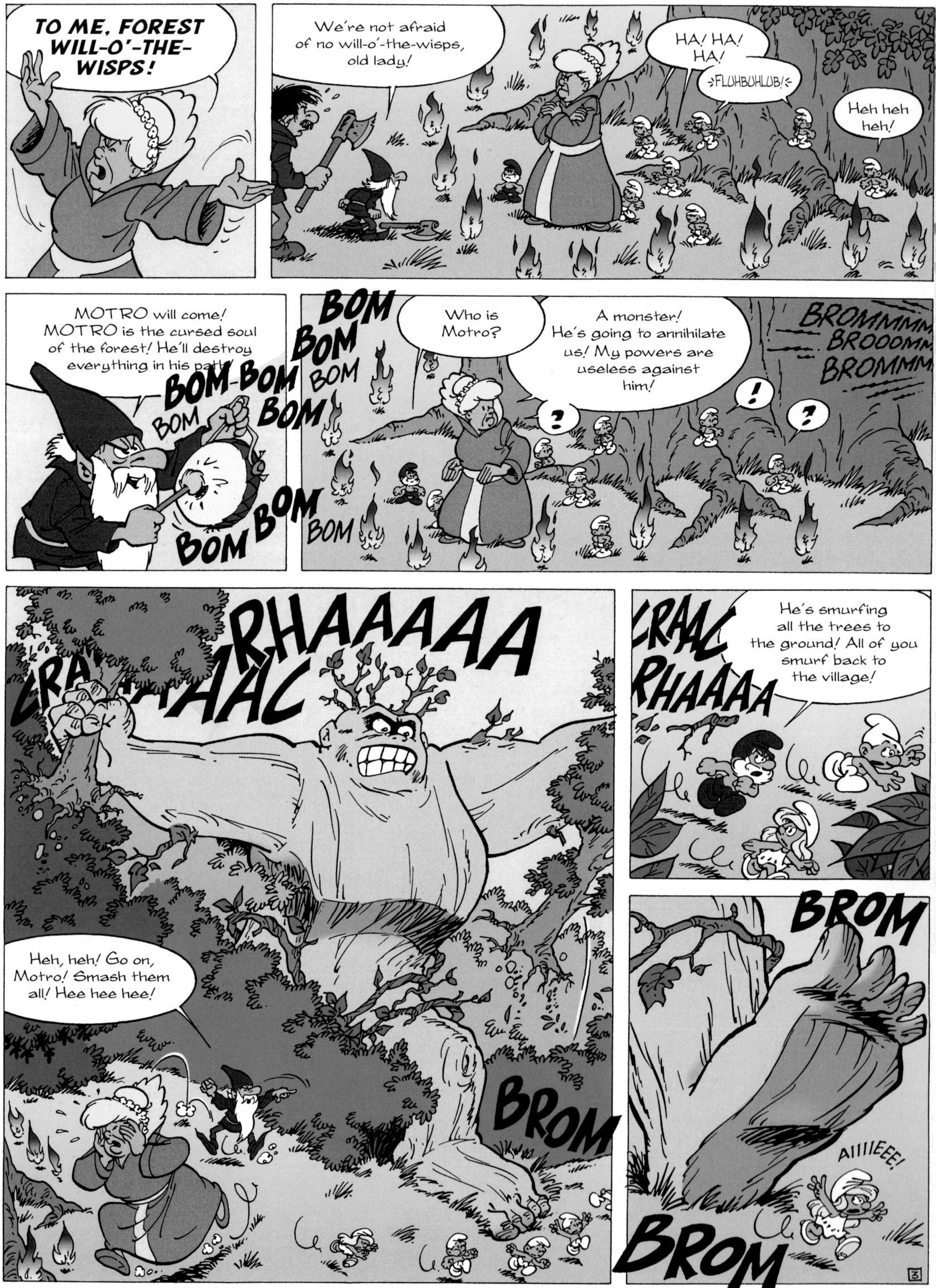
TO ME, FOREST WILL-O'-THE-WISPS!
We're not afraid of no will-o'-the-wisps, old lady!
HA! HA! HA!
FLUHBUHLUB!
Heh heh heh!
MOTRO will come! MOTRO is the cursed soul of the forest! He'll destroy everything in his path!
BOM-BOM BOM BOM BOM BOM BOM BOM BOM BOM BOM BOM
Who is Motro?
A monster! He's going to annihilate us! My powers are useless against him!
?
!
?
BROMMMM BROOOMM BROMMM
RHAAAAAA
AAC
Heh, heh! Go on, Motro! Smash them all! Hee hee hee!
BROM
CRAAC
RHAAAA
He's smurfing all the trees to the ground! All of you smurf back to the village!
BROM
AIIIIEEE!
BROM
3

That way, Motro! Tear out all those trees! Maybe we'll find the village of those idiotic Smurfs, and Gargamel will reward us!

There they are!

CRAA!

RHAAAA

They're pursuing us! He risks smurfing our village!

I have an idea! Smurf me up there!

Look out! There he is! Smurf your all!

We'll get 'em!

Ha ha ha!

RHAAAA

Aah! The traitors! It was a trap!

BONK

Hurray! We did it!

Uh, no! Look!

RHAAAAA

They'll pay for that! Show them no mercy! Capture them all, Motro!

RHAAAA

AAAA

Hiiiii

Only Homnibus can smurf us from that diabolical creature!

BROMBROM

He's coming!

BROM

Don't miss SMURFS MONSTERS, available now at booksellers everywhere!

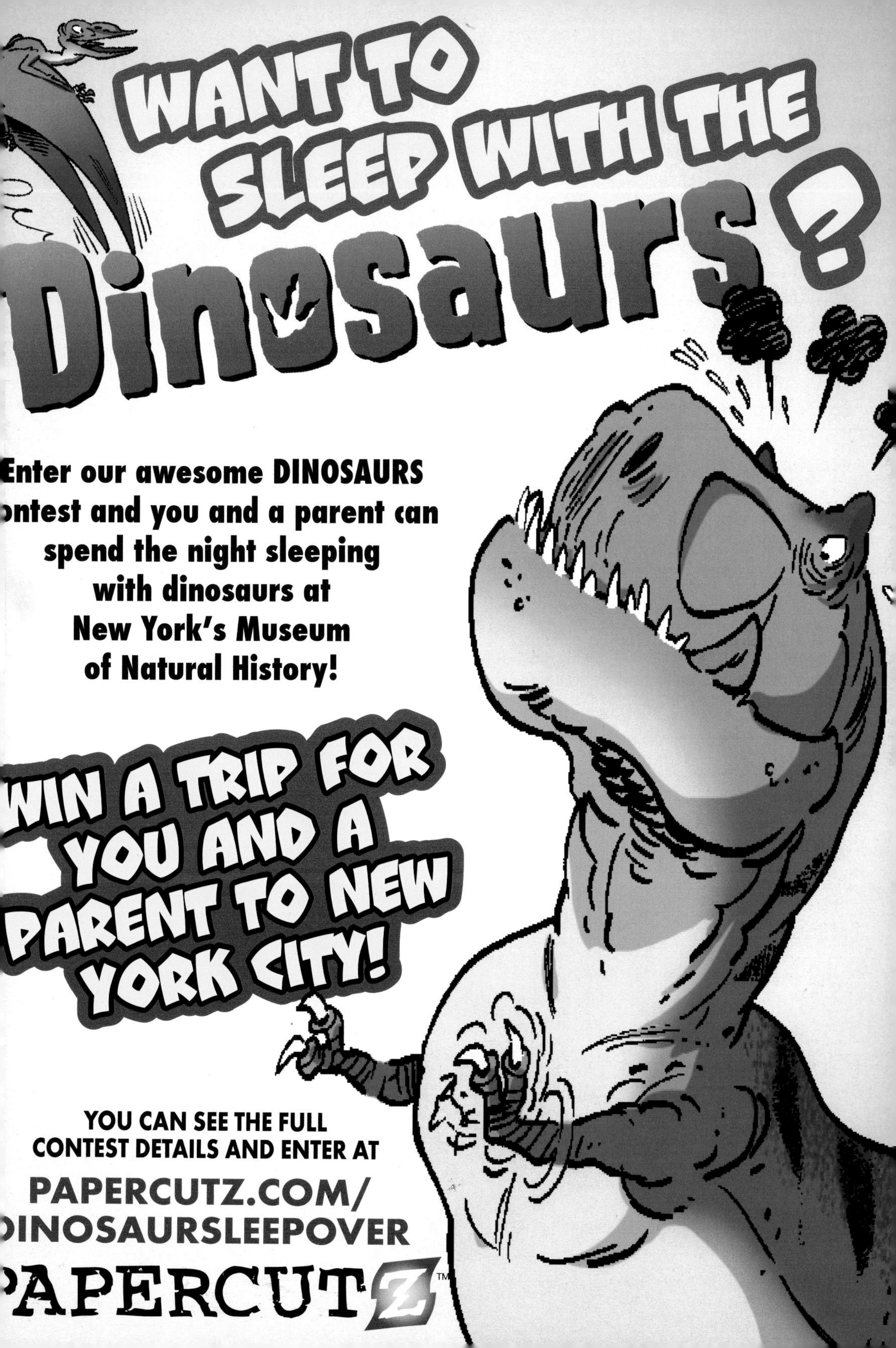

WANT TO SLEEP WITH THE Dinosaurs?
Enter our awesome DINOSAURS
ontest and you and a parent can
spend the night sleeping
with dinosaurs at
New York's Museum
of Natural History!
WIN A TRIP FOR YOU AND A PARENT TO NEW YORK CITY!
YOU CAN SEE THE FULL
CONTEST DETAILS AND ENTER AT
PAPERCUTZ.COM/
DINOSAURSLEEPOVER
PAPERCUTZ™

Index of Terms

Carnivore: an animal that eats meat.

Ceratopsia: the group that includes dinosaurs with frills and horns (such as Triceratops).

Coprolite: fossilized animal droppings.

Cretaceous: era between 145 and 65 million years ago.

Dinosaur: term created by Sir Richard Owen that means "fearfully great lizard." Dinosaurs were reptiles but had their own distinctive characteristics. (For example, they held their legs directly under their bodies.) All dinosaurs were land-based. None flew, and none lived in the water.

Fossil: an animal or vegetable solidified in rock.

Hadrosaurs: the group that includes duck-billed dinosaurs (such as Parasaurolophus).

Herbivore: an animal that lives on plants. The term, "vegetarian," is probably more appropriate than "herbivore," as herbs and grass only appeared a little while after dinosaurs became extinct.

Jurassic: era between 205 and 145 million years ago.

Mammal: an animal with mammary glands, whose females nurse their young.

Omnivore: an animal that eats animals as well as plants.

Ornithischian: a dinosaur with hips like a bird.

Ornithopod: the group that includes many herbivorous dinosaurs, such as Iguanodons.

Paleontology: the science that studies extinct species. Its specialists are paleontologists.

Piscivore: an animal that eats fish.

Plesiosaur: a marine reptile that was almost a dinosaur.

Predator: an animal that attacks its prey to eat it.

Pterosaur: a flying reptile that was almost a dinosaur.

Reptiles: vertebrates that primarily crawl. They currently include crocodiles, lizards, snakes, turtles, and used to include dinosaurs, pterosaurs, and plesiosaurs.

Saurischian: a dinosaur with hips like a lizard.

Sauropod: the group that includes long-neck dinosaurs.

Theropod: the group that includes predatory dinosaurs and birds.

Triassic: era in which dinosaurs appeared, between 250 and 205 million years ago.

G L O S A R Y

Acrocanthosaurus (Page 7)
Meaning: High-spine lizard
Period: Early Cretaceous (110-116 million years ago)
Order/ Family: Saurischia/ Carcharaodontosauridae
Size: 40 feet long (12 meters)
Weight: 7 tons (6350 kilograms)
Diet: Carnivore
Found: United States (Oklahoma, Texas, Utah)

Apatosaurus (Page 5)
Meaning: Deceptive Reptile
Period: Late Jurassic (150-155 million years ago)
Order/ Family: Saurischia/ Diplodocidae
Size: 28 yards long (26 meters)
Weight: 30 tons (27,216 kg)
Diet: Herbivore
Found: United States

Beelzebufo (Page 32)
Meaning: Devil Toad
Period: Late Cretaceous (70 million years ago)
Order/ Family: Anura/ Leptoylidae
Size: 16 inches long (40 cm)
Weight: 9 pounds (4 kg)
Diet: Carnivore
Found: Madagascar

Corythosaurus (Page 26)
Meaning: Helmet lizard
Period: Late Cretaceous (75 million years ago)
Order/ Family: Ornithischia/ Hadrosauridae
Size: 30 feet long (9 meters)
Weight: 4 tons (4 metric tons)
Diet: Herbivore
Found: Canada, United States

Daspletosaurus (Page 35)
Meaning: Frightful lizard
Period: Late Cretaceous (72-80 million years ago)
Order/ Family: Saurischia/ Tyrannosauridae
Size: 30 feet long (9 meters)
Weight: 4 tons (4 metric tons)
Diet: Carnivore
Found: United States (Montana) and Canada (Alberta)

Gigantoraptor (Page 15)
Meaning: Giant seizer
Period: Late Cretaceous (70 million years ago)
Order/ Family: Saurischia/ Oviraptidae
Size: 26 feet long (8 meters)
Weight: 4,409 pounds (2 metric tons)
Diet: Herbivore?
Found: Mongolia

Guanlong (Page 30)
Meaning: Crowned dragon
Period: Late Jurassic (160 million years ago)
Order/ Family: Saurischia/ Proceratosauridae
Size: 10 feet long (3 meters)
Weight: 198 pounds (90 kg)
Diet: Carnivore
Found: China

Ichthyovenator (Page 3)
Meaning: Fish Hunter
Period: Early Cretaceous (112-125 million years ago)
Order/ Family: Saurischia/ Spinosauridae
Size: 27 feet long (8 meters)
Weight: 1 ton (907 kg)
Diet: Piscivore
Found: Laos

Lythronax (Page 38)
Meaning: Gore King
Period: Late Cretaceous (80 million years ago)
Order/ Family: Saurischia/ Tyrannosauridae
Size: 26 feet long (8 meters)
Weight: 5,512 pounds (2.5 metric tons)
Diet: Carnivore
Found: United States (Utah)

Majungasaurus (Page 23)
Meaning: Mahajanga (province of Madagascar) lizard
Period: Late Cretaceous (65-70 million years ago)
Order/ Family: Saurischia/ Abelisauridae
Size: 30 feet long (9 meters)
Weight: 2,205 pounds (1 metric ton)
Diet: Carnivore
Found: Madagascar

GLOSSARY

Massospondylus (Page 20)
Meaning: Longer vertebrae
Period: Early Jurassic (183-200 million years ago)
Order/ Family: Saurischia/ Massospondydae
Size: 13 feet long (4 meters)
Weight: 441 pounds (200 kilograms)
Diet: Herbivore
Found: South Africa, Lesotho, United States (?)

Mosasaurus (Page 18)
Meaning: Meuse River Lizard
Period: Late Cretaceous (65-70 million years ago)
Order/ Family: Squamata/ Mosauridae
Size: 59 feet long (18 meters)
Weight: 16.5 tons (15 metric tons)
Diet: Piscivore
Found: The whole world

Nanotyrannus (Page 12)
Meaning: Dwarf tyrant
Period: Late Cretaceous (65 million years ago)
Order/ Family: Saurischia/ Tyrannosauridae
Size: 20 feet (6 meters long)
Weight: 2205 pounds (1 metric ton)
Diet: Carnivore
Fossils: United States (Montana)

Nigersaurus (Page 40)
Meaning: Niger reptile
Period: Early Jurassic (110-118 million years ago)
Order/ Family: Saurischia/ Rebbbachisauridae
Size: 49 feet long (15 meters)
Weight: 4 tons (4 metric tons)
Diet: Herbivore
Found: Africa (Niger)

Pegomastax (Page 8)
Meaning: Strong jaw
Period: Early Jurassic (183-200 million years ago)
Order/ Family: Ornithischia/ Heterodontosauridae
Size: 2 feet (60 centimeters long)
Weight: 55 pounds (25 kg)
Diet: Herbivore
Found: South Africa

Sauroniops (Page 25)
Meaning: Eye of Sauron
Period: Late Cretaceous (93-99 million years ago)
Order/ Family: Saurischia/ Charcharodontosauridae
Size: 39 feet long (12 meters)
Weight: 6.6 tons? (6 metric tons?)
Diet: Carnivore
Found: North Africa (Morocco)

Scipionyx (Page 29)
Meaning: Scipio's claw
Period: Early Cretaceous (113 million years ago)
Order/ Family: Saurischia/ Compsognathidae
Size: 1.5 feet long (45 centimeters) (baby)/ 7 feet long
(2 meters) (adult)
Weight: 11 ounces (300 grams) (baby)/ 88 pounds (40 kg)
(adult)
Diet: Carnivore, Piscivore
Found: Italy

Scutellosaurus (Page 17)
Meaning: Little-shielded lizard
Period: Early Jurassic (190-200 million years ago)
Order/ Family: Ornithischia/ Thyreophora
Size: 4 feet long (1.2 meters)
Weight: 22 pounds (10 kg)
Diet: Herbivore
Found: United States (Arizona)

Styracosaurus (Page 36)
Meaning: Spiked lizard
Period: Late Cretaceous (72-80 million years ago)
Order/ Family: Ornithischia/ Certapsia
Size: 16 feet long (5 meters)
Weight: 6,614 pounds (3 metric tons)
Diet: Herbivore
Found: United States, Canada

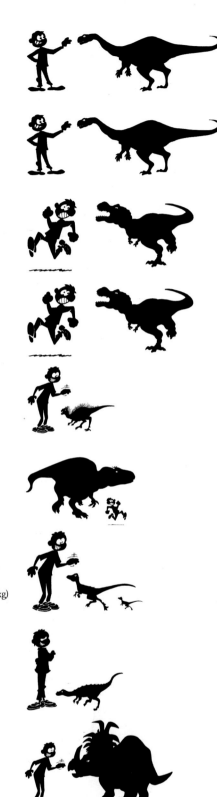

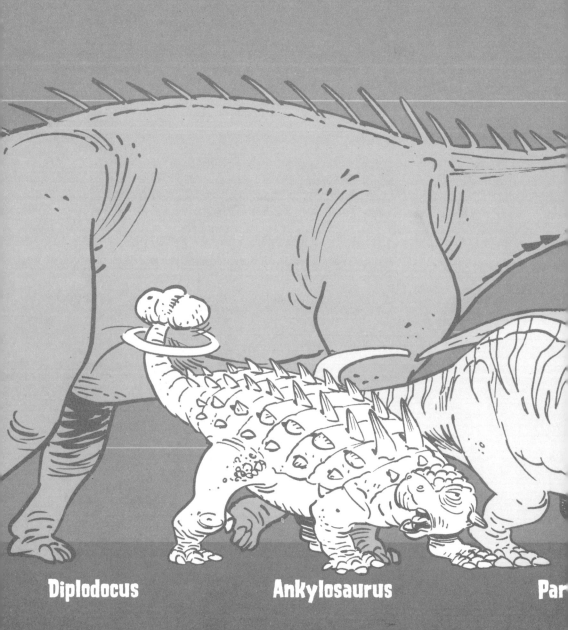

Diplodocus　　　　　**Ankylosaurus**　　　　　**Par**